TWO CANES ON THE TUNDRA

MARY TELLEFSON

Two Canes on the Tundra
Copyrighted © 2021 Mary Tellefson
ISBN 9781645383215
First Edition

Two Canes on the Tundra
by Mary Tellefson
With illustrations by Destine Poulsen
Some modifications and coloring created by Mary Tellefson
and Jayden Ellsworth

All Rights Reserved. Written permission must be secured from the publisher to use or reproduce any part of this book, except for brief quotations in critical reviews or articles.

For information, please contact:

www.orangehatpublishing.com
Waukesha, WI

This book is dedicated to little kids who use canes, and adult cane users who were once little kids.

Happy Reading

Mary T.

Chapter One:
Apu and A Rotten-Walrus Cousin

Standing at the river's edge in their Alaskan Yupik village (*nunat*), eleven-year-old Apu was holding on to the arm of his twelve-year old cousin, (*iluracungaq*) Brink.

"The salmon are running! I hear a lot of splashing," shouted Apu. "Do you see a lot of red?"

"All over the place, but especially close to the bank," replied Brink who was accustomed to explaining what he could see to his blind, younger cousin. He was also responsible for guiding Apu on his arm to and from school (*elitnaurvik*). They often stopped at the river on their way home. Brink continued, "Maybe we can come fishing with Grandfather (*Apa'urluq*) tomorrow after school. He will be so pleased the salmon finally arrived."

"The whole village will be happy to eat salmon all winter," added Apu.

No one knew for sure why the salmon were spawning so late in the season. The fish usually made their way up the Kuskokwim river in late June and into July to lay their eggs, but it was already late August. *I wonder if it has anything to do with global warming*, thought Apu.

Responding to Brink's idea, Apu replied, "I'm sure Grandfather will want to fish with us. We don't have Native Drumming Club after school so we're good to go. He should be getting home from his doctor appointment in Anchorage any minute." After a tiny pause, "Well what good timing. I hear his plane coming in now," said Apu, smiling.

While they looked out over the water, Apu felt and heard Brink twist his whole body so he could look up at the airplane (*tengssuun*) overhead. Brink tipped his head back so far, his hat fell off and he lost his balance, almost ending up in the river.

Apu laughed. *He's been kind of clumsy all day*, he thought to himself. *Wouldn't be the first time I almost ended up in the water because of him.*

While Brink watched the airplane, Apu turned his head so his ear was in a better position to hear a different sound behind them. He heard the eerie warning call of a loon (*qaleqcuuq*) coming from the lake over the hill. *One of my favorite sounds in the whole world.* He knew Brink would soon be able to see what was causing the loon to sound its warning.

Apu turned toward Brink and said, "Watch for the bald eagle (*yaqulpak*) behind us." Brink turned around and saw the eagle soaring high above the tundra (*nunapik*).

"How did you know an eagle was up there when you can't even see? Did you hear it?" asked Brink.

Apu smiled, feeling proud. "I didn't hear the eagle, but I did hear the warning call of a loon. Remember Grandfather teaching us that whenever a loon sees an eagle, it cries a special warning to other loons to protect their babies? Just because I'm blind doesn't mean I don't know what's going on around me, Brink."

Apu shifted his attention toward the dirt landing strip on the east side of the village where the twin-engine airplane was beginning to land. He was excited to hear the high-pitched whine of the engine as the plane slowed down. His shoulders tightened, expecting the explosion of dirt and gravel as the tires hit the runway. Letting go of Brink's arm, Apu pointed toward the airplane.

"I hope he got help for his bad knee." As Apu reached for Brink's arm again, Brink moved away so Apu missed his arm and grabbed nothing but air. Brink laughed, causing Apu to yell, "Geez, Brink, you're a rotten-walrus (*asveq*) cousin."

"I am a great cousin. Don't I take you everywhere you need to go? To school? To the community center? To the fishing hole? To the wharf?" countered Brink.

Apu didn't know who he felt worse for, himself or Brink. He hated the jokes Brink played on him, like pulling his arm away. But he also realized that Brink didn't have a choice about being his guide around the village. Taking care of family was expected. When Brink wasn't available, his younger sister, Hitty, had guide duty, and that was totally embarrassing. The other boys teased him relentlessly when they saw him hanging on to his little sister's arm. Being guided by Brink was better than that, even if Brink did play rotten jokes on him once in a while—like now.

I wish I could just walk home on my own and leave you here, Brink. I know my way, but it might not be worth the risk of falling off the boardwalk and breaking my leg again since I can't see the edge. Or running into a moose or bear. I'm not brave enough for that. But if I was...

Apu often thought about bravery. He grew up hearing stories of his brave ancestors (*ciuliat*) who followed their food sources through the Alaskan wilderness. Grandfather made the stories come alive in Apu's mind, and Apu would imagine himself as the proud and brave character in the story, hunting and whaling in the Arctic Circle. But in this moment, he was dependent on his almost-same-age cousin to guide him home.

Apu's mind drifted back to earlier in the day when a new teacher (*elitnaurista*) showed up at school wanting to teach him to use a mobility cane (*ayaruq*). Even with the promise of getting around the village without needing a guide, it hadn't gone well. But in this moment, frustrated with Brink, he thought, *maybe I should give it chance. . . .* but shut down the thought. He sighed, "C'mon Brink, let me take your arm. Let's head home to greet Grandfather."

Chapter Two:
I Don't Want It

Thinking about Grandfather always made Apu and Brink feel proud. He was a village elder (*tegganeq*), famous for carving real-looking animals, trees, and village scenes from wood and walrus ivory. Grandfather learned to carve from his father who learned to carve from his father. In this way, the craft was passed down several generations among the males. Now, Grandfather was teaching both boys to carve. *I hope Grandfather was able to get the special carving knives (mellgaq) we need while he was in Anchorage,* thought Apu as they approached their home.

The boys arrived home just as Grandfather was pulling up in the four-wheeler with his small suitcase strapped on the back. Their home had two good-sized bedrooms that his grandparents and parents used, a smaller third bedroom for Hitty and his younger brother Harvey to share, and an add-on room where Apu and Brink shared a bunkbed and closet. Sharing a room with Brink was challenging because he threw his dirty clothes, shoes, and other stuff all over the floor for Apu to step on or trip over.

How many times had Apu told Brink, "Keep your things picked up! Do you see how my stuff is organized in boxes on the closet floor, and my clothes are on hangers? That's what the closet is for, Brink. You should give it a try." But it never did any good.

Now, standing in the kitchen waiting for Grandfather, Apu slowly became aware of a smell that was making his mouth water. Grandmother (*maurluq*) was making a special dinner for Grandfather's return. *That's got to be baked salmon with high bush cranberry sauce,* Apu identified. Another familiar smell made his nose quiver in delight. "Fry bread smells great, Grandmother," he complimented.

"Thanks, Honey," Grandmother answered. "Did you stop by the river on your way home? Were the salmon running?"

"Yep. We want Grandfather to fish with us tomorrow after school."

"You might even get out of school for fishing," replied Grandmother. "Maybe school will be cancelled so the whole village can fish."

As Grandfather entered the kitchen, Apu wasn't sure if he heard or smelled him first. Exhaust fumes from the four-wheeler clinging to Grandfather's clothes announced his presence. Apu didn't like the smell much.

"Hi, everyone," greeted Grandfather. Walking over to the stove, he put his hand on Grandmother's shoulder and sniffed the salmon, saying, "Smells wonderful, and I'm famished. I'll wash up quick so we can eat."

"I'm hungry, too," said Apu as he took his regular place at the table. He heard a chorus of, *me too*, from Brink, Hitty, Harvey, Mom, and Dad, and he just knew Grandmother was smiling.

Grandfather blessed the meal, thanking the earth for providing food as it had for their ancestors who had traveled over many miles each year to hunt and fish for food. As they began to eat, Grandfather asked the question he always asked at supper time. "What happened at school today, kids?"

Hitty replied, "I forgot my lunch, but Ada shared hers with me."

"That was nice of her," said her mother. "You thanked her, right?"

"Yep," replied Hitty.

"I don't go to school yet," said Harvey with a mouth full of fry bread. "But I helped Momma pick berries for pie."

Brink answered next, "Nothing new with me, Grandfather. Same as every day."

Frowning and making a small snorting sound through his nose, Apu answered last. "I have a new teacher, Mr. Alan. He came from Anchorage. He gave me a mobility cane and made me walk down the school hallways with it in front of everybody. It was so stupid and embarrassing. The other kids teased me and got in my way on purpose, jumping back and forth over it until Mr. Alan yelled at them."

Mr. Alan was a special teacher who taught blind children how to use a cane while they walked or moved around so they didn't bump into things they couldn't see and get hurt. He wanted to teach Apu to use the mobility cane instead of hanging on to someone's arm all the time. But Apu was mad about being teased, so at the end of the day, when he left school to go home, he hid the cane in the custodian's closet, hoping it would magically disappear.

"Tell me more," invited Grandfather.

Apu wished he didn't have to talk about it, and

he sure wasn't going to say he ditched the cane at school, but it would be disrespectful not to answer. He cleared his throat. "Ah, Mr. Alan is an 'orientation and mobility' instructor. He says 'O&M' means knowing where you are, where you want to go, and being able to get there. He wants to teach me how to use a cane so I can go places by

myself without getting hurt. He said it will help me be independent and give me choices."

Apu stopped talking and was deciding whether or not to repeat the whole conversation, which he really preferred not to do, when Grandfather said, "Go on."

Rats. "So, he gave me a lesson with it, and the kids were obnoxious, and I told him I wasn't interested in using it."

"What did he say to that?" asked Grandmother.

"He explained that it was a tool (*angicissun*) and asked me about tools we use at our house, like what traditional tool Grandmother uses to cut up fish and meat. I told him an uluaq. Then he asked me what tool Grandfather uses to make his beautiful carvings." Apu took a loud breath, "Then he asked me what tool the family uses to keep the floor clean. He said that Grandmother's ulu, Grandfather's knives, and the broom are tools that serve a special purpose, and the mobility cane is a special tool, too, and that I shouldn't be embarrassed to use a tool."

"What makes it embarrassing, Apu?" asked his mom.

Apu was silent. *I am so tired of trying to explain things to people who don't understand what it's like to be different than everyone else. To need so much help. I'm the only one in the whole village who is blind.*

Grandfather took charge again. He often used situations like this to teach the children about their culture. "What if your ancestors were too embarrassed to use the tools they created for survival, like ulus, harpoons (*tegun*), and spears? How would they have gotten food? None of us would be here today." Grandfather paused. "I like the idea that a mobility cane is a tool. Apu, we all use tools. The doctor in Anchorage gave me a walking cane, a tool to use for my bad knee. It helps me a lot. Let's talk with Mr. Alan together tomorrow. I'd hate for you to pass up this opportunity. In the past you've talked about wishing you could be more independent."

Whatever, thought Apu. *At least I'll get out of class for a while.*

Chapter Three:
"Come Make Fun of Me Now"

The next day, Apu was jittery as he waited in the school office for his Grandfather to arrive. Mr. Alan was trying to have a conversation with him, but he felt too nervous to say much. *Wish I was fishing instead of doing this. But tomorrow is the fishing day.* Finally, Apu heard Grandfather's uneven footsteps limp into the office.

"Hi, Grandfather," said Apu. "This is Mr. Alan."

After they exchanged greetings and Mr. Alan thanked Grandfather for coming, he jumped right into an explanation of the mobility cane. Smiling, he said, "Basically, the mobility cane is a tool that helps blind people know what's in front of them and if their next step will be safe. For example, if the ground is not level or if there is a step up or down, the mobility cane would find it so Apu wouldn't stumble or trip."

While Mr. Alan continued to explain, Apu allowed his mind to imagine. *Independent? I wonder what it would be like to ditch Brink. No, I don't mean it in a mean way. What would it be like if I walked to school by myself, or with Brink but not hanging on to him? I think I would like Brink better. Maybe he would like me better. I could walk away when we argue or if he's being mean.*

Apu tuned back into what Mr. Alan was saying. "Sometimes, there are things left in the hallway Apu could walk into and injure himself. Just yesterday, I saw a bucket full of water left outside the boys' bathroom. The custodian was mopping the floor and left the bucket by the door." He turned to Apu. "If you had been on your way to the bathroom at that time, you probably would have walked right into it."

Apu couldn't help frowning a little. *Really? We're going to talk about me going to the bathroom as the example? Can you humiliate me any more than that?*

"If you use a mobility cane, it will give you a warning before you bump into something, then you can walk *around* it instead of *into* it," finished Mr. Alan.

Nodding his head, Grandfather asked Apu, "What benefits do you see, Apu?"

Apu hesitated. *Can I please just go back to class?* "Well, I guess I'd know where the edge of the boardwalk is and wouldn't be afraid of falling off."

Mr. Alan added, "And especially when you need to move over to let a four-wheeler past, you'd know exactly where the edge was." The village didn't have any streets or cars, only boardwalks, four-wheelers and snow-machines in winter. Dog sleds were used outside the village to cross open ground.

One point for Mr. Alan, thought Apu. *I prefer not to break my leg falling off the edge.* He remembered the time he did fall off when he was five years old. He sprained his ankle and ended up in a cast. *I'm not up for that again.*

Apu heard Mr. Alan unzip his backpack. He recognized the sound of the aluminum sections of a folding cane being extended to its full length.

Yikes, he must have found it in the closet. I hope he doesn't tell Grandfather I hid it. He felt the cane being put in his hand.

"Show your Grandfather what I taught you yesterday."

All of a sudden, Apu felt his face get hot in anger. He wanted to leave. He felt like he was being forced to say how good the cane would work for him when he didn't feel good about it. *Why don't they get it? What about the teasing I got from the other kids yesterday?* Tattling on them would just make it worse. He felt stuck. "You can show him, and I'll listen," replied Apu, giving the cane back.

Apu didn't see Grandfather raise his eyebrows or the look shared between him and Mr. Alan. They could see how uncomfortable Apu was getting. They ignored his tone and moved on.

"Sure, I can do that," said Mr. Alan as he stepped behind Grandfather. He put the cane in Grandfather's hand, and showed him how to move it back and forth, first on his right side, then on his left side in front of him.

"When the cane is tapped back and forth like this, touching the tip on the floor on each side of the body, we call it *touch technique*. It will bump into anything in Apu's path to let him know there is something in the way that he could trip over. He will be able to feel edges and detect drop-offs or steps. As you can guess, it wouldn't protect his head. So if there was a bush branch sticking out, or if someone left a cabinet door open, the

cane would not find it before his head did. It only protects its user from the waist down to the floor."

"I see," replied Grandfather.

With a chuckle in his voice, Mr. Alan added, "Could scare a moose off the boardwalk too."

Or get me kicked in the head, thought Apu. Occasionally a moose would wander onto the boardwalk and villagers would get the word out. They weren't an animal to mess with, especially a female with a calf.

"Thank you for your time, Mr. Alan," said Grandfather. "Apu, grab your cane and head back to class. We'll talk more at home."

Reluctantly, Apu did what he was told. He hated the idea of being seen with it. It was like shouting, *"Hey everyone. I'm different. Come make fun of me now." On the other hand, is that better or worse than being teased for holding on to Hitty?* Confused, he headed back to class.

Chapter Four:
Two Canes on the Tundra

That evening while eating spaghetti with reindeer meatballs for dinner, Grandfather turned to Apu, who was very quiet. "I know today was uncomfortable for you. Did you have another lesson with Mr. Alan?"

"Yes," whispered Apu with his head down.

"So, what's the problem?"

"I'm not sure it's worth the teasing."

"Well, maybe answering some questions will help. How do you walk to school without falling off the boardwalks?"

"I hold on to Brink's arm."

"Do you ever get upset with Brink and wish you could walk away on your own?"

"Mmhmm," voiced Apu as he heard Brink starting to squirm in his chair.

"Do you ever wish you didn't have to wait for Brink when he is running late for school?"

"Yes, and I wish he wouldn't leave stupid stuff on the floor in the bedroom for me to trip over."

Grandfather looked at Brink, who shrugged his shoulders but stayed silent.

Back to Apu, "Do you ever wish you didn't have to walk with Hitty when Brink isn't around?

"Yes," said Apu. "I get teased *a lot* because she's my little sister. No offense, Hitty. But Grandfather, I also got teased using the cane."

Hearing this, Hitty shrugged her shoulders as she had seen Brink do.

"It takes courage to face challenges, Apu. Just like your ancestors faced challenges to their wellbeing and overcame them, you will face and overcome yours. You will be stronger and feel proud of yourself. Even if you have to put up with a little teasing, it sounds like the mobility cane is the right tool for you, just like my support cane is the right tool for my hurt knee."

Apu's brain felt crushed with a thousand negative feelings, but hearing Grandfather mention ancestors and his own cane made him feel curious. He hadn't given much thought to his grandfather's new cane.

"Can I take a look at your cane?" he asked.

Grandfather got his walking cane from the corner by the door. He put it in Apu's hands. As Apu felt it from the handle down to the tip, he commented on each discovery. "It's shorter than mine and fatter. Mine is skinnier. Yours is made of wood, mine is aluminum. Your handle is different than mine, too. Oh, yours has a rubber tip."

"That's because mine is for leaning on," Grandfather explained.

Apu asked, "Did you carve this feather hanging off the handle?"

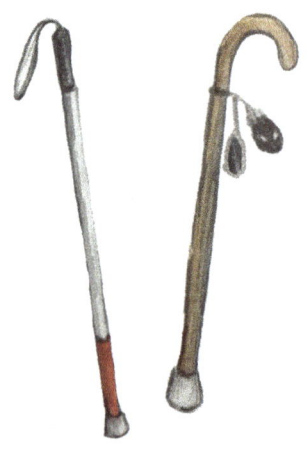

Grandfather answered, "Yes, a black and white one from one of your favorite birds."

"A loon!" exclaimed Apu.

"Yes, a loon. As a mother loon carries her babies on her back to keep them safe, this walking stick keeps me safe by taking weight off my knee. It lessens the chance of my knee giving out and landing me on the ground. Now, that would be embarrassing."

Apu moved his hand further down the shaft of the walking cane, feeling gently for what came next. He had learned to use a soft touch when he learned to read and write Braille. He fingered some beads that were strung together in the shape of a small rectangle.

"What is this, Grandfather?"

"It is what remains of a good luck charm (*iinruq*) my grandmother, your great-grandmother, made as a gift to me for my first whale hunt."

Brink interrupted, "And before getting to be one of the hunters, you were only allowed to bail water out of the boat and serve the hunters coffee, right, Grandfather?"

"Yes, and finally, when I was a real hunter, the good luck charm did bring me luck. We harvested a bowhead whale west of Nunivak Island that fed the village all winter long."

I could use a good luck charm about now, thought Apu.

Grandfather continued, "Everything you see on my support cane is special to me. I can help you decorate your cane with what is special to you, Apu." *Cool. I have some special things inside my nature box . . . if Brink hasn't totally destroyed the closet with his junk,* thought Apu.

"First, we'll have a remembering and blessing ceremony to help you appreciate your new tool. On Friday evening, our whole family will participate, and we will invite Mr. Alan, too. Bring your cane to the ceremony, Apu."

"Ok, Grandfather," sighed Apu as he picked up his fork.

Chapter Five:
The Ceremony

Two days later, Apu sat with his family in lawn chairs around the fire pit in the backyard, waiting for Grandfather to begin. Apu, Brink, Hitty, and Harvey were excited. They enjoyed the ceremonies Grandfather created to teach them about their culture and their ancestors. But he wasn't the only storyteller. *I hope Grandmother tells my favorite story,* he thought.

Grandfather started the ceremony by explaining that the children would have a turn using their imaginations to bless Apu's cane right after the adults. He lit the fire, and when it was burning high, he threw in a few twigs of spruce to perfume the air. Apu took a deep breath as Grandfather, noticing the northern lights, lowered his eyes

and whispered, "I honor our ancestors, who for nearly three thousand years survived the Alaskan wilderness using only the tools they could make for themselves from resources that nature provided. We are a strong, brave, and capable people of the land. Our hearts are filled with appreciation as we call upon the spirit of our ancestors to help us do what is necessary to live our best lives in harmony with the natural world. Are we living our best lives? Apu, please hand me your cane."

Silently, Apu reached his cane toward his Grandfather's voice. Grandfather took the cane from him and held it for all to see. He turned it diagonally.

"Apu, to you this object is a cane. But in my mind's eye, it is a tool for successful hunting. It is a harpoon that, before we had guns, our people used to hunt seals, walrus, and whales. It took courage for a fleet of kayaks made from wood and animal skins to approach a whale. One flip of its mighty tale could overturn the kayaks and injure or kill the team of hunters. Even today, when guns are used, a harpoon with a float attached is used to make sure our catch doesn't sink before we can get it bound for towing. Without the harpoon, your ancestors would have gone hungry. Apu, like

the harpoon, this cane is a tool that offers the gifts of courage and success to accomplish important tasks in your life, like feeding your family and village."

Apu smiled, remembering a time a whale had beached up on this part of the river. "*Grandfather*," he had practically screamed, "*a whale beached itself down by the airport beach. I want to go see it.*" The whole family had hurried down to the river's edge. It was a very unusual circumstance since whales live in the deeper ocean, not the river. I can't believe how huge it is, he had thought to himself as he walked completely around the carcass, experiencing the massive bulk of skin and understanding its size. *To hunt a whale with harpoons takes an amount of bravery equal to the whale's size*, he concluded. *What is a little teasing compared to that?*

Grandfather passed the cane to his left, where Grandmother took it in her callused hands. Grandmother was known for telling the longest stories. She turned the cane parallel to the ground and took a deep breath. She let it out slowly.

Anticipating his favorite story, Apu shivered with goosebumps. He often imagined himself as his great-great-uncle, the main character of this adventure.

Grandmother began, "Apu, to you this object is a cane, but in my mind's eye, it is a runner on the dog sled that carried the mail to the villages before the time of airplanes. In 1923, my great-uncle (*ataata*) was a musher (*qimugciurta*). He delivered mail up and down the Yukon River to other villages before the mail planes existed. The mail run was an important job because it was the only way to get medicine to the villages where people were sick. He would be gone for weeks at a time, staying at roadhouses along the way. I can still remember the names of all eight malamutes on his dog team.

"When he was getting ready for a mail run, he would put moose hide booties on his dog's feet to keep their feet from being cut on jagged ice along the way. The dogs would get so excited. Their yips and howls nearly made us deaf."

Apu felt Grandmother's body relax as she took

a long breath, exhaling through her nose. "Sleds were very heavy at that time, not like the ones we have today. They often carried more than six hundred pounds of the mail, dog food, and other supplies the musher needed.

The sled runners were made of spruce wood as straight as this cane, but curved up at the ends. These were good in the cold, dry snow. But if those curved ends got buried in deep fluffy snow, it could cause the sled to tip over." At the same time Grandmother said the next words out loud, Apu said them in his head. "Wouldn't you know, that's exactly what happened on a cold October day in 1924."

Apu felt his muscles tighten as he anticipated the next part of the story. "Great-Uncle was still ten miles out from the nearest village when the accident happened. You see, when the sled tipped over, his foot was caught under it. He was in a lot of pain, and his foot was bleeding right through his boot from a large cut.

Yikes, I'm bleeding, imagined Apu as he unconsciously rubbed his foot.

Grandma continued, "He knew if he took his boot off, his foot would swell up and he wouldn't get it back on and he would get frostbite. He had an ice pick in the sled, another tool, and he used it to push himself to a standing position. Hopping on one foot, he ordered the dogs here and there while he got the sled right side up on the runners. His team was ready to run again, but Great-Uncle was feeling like he might faint. He didn't give up, though. No, he knew people were depending on him to bring the mail and medicines they were waiting for."

Apu took a lung full of the spruce-perfumed air, puffing out his chest and holding it there. *What if someone is depending on me? Could I get help for them? I could . . . if I could get around on my own.* He let out the air.

"Great-Uncle made a place on the sled where he could lay down and covered himself up as best he could with skins and blankets to stay warm. He yelled 'hike' to his team. He trusted his dogs knew the route to the next village. They took off howling, and that's the last he heard until loud voices woke

him up. He opened his eyes to find a circle of eyes looking down at him. Thank goodness those eyes belonged to people and not to wolves (*keglunret*). His dogs had made it to the village after he fainted. The village people took care of his injury and fed him hot moose stew. He became a hero for his persistence in bringing the mail."

Apu was imagining a circle of wolves looking down at him. *I'm not afraid of you. I feel your warm breath on my face. It's smelly. Have you just eaten? Good, I am not willing to be your dinner.* He could sense their curiosity but surprisingly felt brave and confident.

Grandmother turned the cane perpendicular to the floor, straight up and down with the handle in the air and the tip on the ground. "Apu, if you receive it, this cane, like the runner on Great-Uncle's dog sled, offers the gift of persistence in traveling to where you want or need to go. People can depend on you to show up when it is important."

Apu blinked back tears as Mother took the cane from Grandmother. She closed her eyes, a smile lighting up her face. She reached up briefly to feel the walrus bone necklace she was wearing, then she put both hands back on the cane.

"Apu, to you this object is a cane, but in my mind's eye, it is an asking stick! During the yearly *Asking Festival*, a man would let his family know the gifts he wished to receive by making models of them and hanging them from a carved stick.

"One year, my oldest sister's husband wished to receive a new pair of mukluks. I was fourteen at the time and old enough to help my sister make them. It is a complicated process.

"The bottom or sole of the mukluk was made from the dried skin of a bearded seal, which is waterproof. It was hard work to cut the pattern with an ulu and scrape all the fur, dried blubber, and oil off. My hands ached at the end of the day, but we still had to trim and attach the caribou hide to make the top part of the mukluk that reached to the knees.

"I was especially pleased when my sister asked me to add my own beadwork and feathers to decorate them." Again, she touched the necklace she was wearing. "Sister's husband loved them and gave us each a walrus bone necklace and earrings to show his appreciation."

Mother touched Apu's hand. "Apu, if you receive it, your cane, like an *asking stick*, is a tool that reminds you that you can ask for what you want so you can live your best life. When you ask, you must be ready for the answer. As you grow up, you will want different things at different times. Remember that the Asking Festival teaches us to show appreciation to the people who help us along the way, too. I think your teacher is one of those people."

I have asked to be like other kids in the way they can go around the village without hanging on to a cousin or little sister, thought Apu. *Mother wants me to see that the cane is my answer and I need to be willing to use it. I do get it now, but I want the teasing to stop.*

Apu felt the stirring of a breeze on his face. He listened for the firewood to snap and pop. He was ready to move out of the smoke if the breeze blew it his way. He heard Hitty yawn and understood. All the emotion and thinking were making him tired, too.

Mother handed Apu's cane to Father, who was next.

"Apu, to you this object is a cane, but in my mind's eye, it is a fishing rod (*manaq*). My father, who is your grandfather, taught me how to fish for king crabs by making a hole in the ice and dropping a line down. Fishing together with you is special to me, just like fishing with me was special to your grandfather. It is where you and I see the world in the same way.

"Yes, I know you don't see with your eyes. You see with your heart and hands. You see through listening, and you see in your mind's eye, using your imagination. You learned to manage all parts of fishing by yourself, from baiting the hook to casting, landing, and unhooking your catch. But it took time and practice, right? Remember how many times you stuck yourself with the hook? We teased you a little bit, but you just ignored us and kept at it. Now, you can put food on our table with what you catch by yourself.

"Apu, if you receive it, like this fishing rod, your cane is a tool that gives the gift of shared activities with people you care about. It also connects you to your ancestors, who created tools to survive."

Apu felt a big release of emotion. It was like he had been holding his breath and finally, he could breathe again. *I guess the teasing isn't all that bad, and I could ignore it.*

Mr. Alan was the last of the adults to speak. "Apu, to you and to me, this is a mobility cane. In my mind's eye, I see you getting around the village mostly on your own if you want to. I see you walking around things in your way, stepping over ruts, and finding the edge of the boardwalk to make way for four-wheelers. I see you safe and sound with the freedom to make choices you couldn't before. The cane is a tool that, used correctly, gives the gifts of choice and safety. You decide where you want to go and how you want to participate in your family and community, all the while staying safe. You have the opportunity to learn how to use it and receive the gift of safety and choice."

Mr. Alan handed the cane back to Apu and patted him on the back. Apu hugged the cane to his body as if it was a new gift. In the quiet, while he was appreciating all the stories he heard, Brink grabbed the cane out of his hand and started sweeping it like a hockey stick. *Good grief. Leave it to Brink to turn something serious into a joke.* "To you this is a cane, Apu, but to me, it is the hockey stick that slams the winning goal. This cane helps you be a winner, like me."

Suddenly, Hitty grabbed the cane from Brick and used it as an umbrella, pretending the rain was pounding down. Before she could think of any gifts it could give, Harvey snatched it and held it to his mouth like a flute (*cupsaraq*). He squeaked musical notes out of his throat while kicking his legs out at the same time in a silly dance.

Apu laughed along with everyone and released one final yawn. The ceremony was over, Mr. Alan walked back to the school where he was sleeping overnight, and everyone else went inside to bed.

In the bedroom, Apu tripped over Brink's shoes which were left in the middle of the floor. "Good grief, Brink," yawned Apu. "Move your shoes to the closet."

All was quiet as they drifted off to sleep, dreaming of harpooning whales, fishing for king crabs through the ice, making mukluks, and dog sledding with ancestors in the recent and distant past.

Chapter Six:
Freedom

During the next month, Grandfather kept his promise to help Apu decorate his cane. He carved a loon's head out of whalebone that could slip over the mobility cane's handle. A bright red bead made the loon's eye, and a small hole in the top of its head allowed the elastic loop to come out the top. Apu chose several items out of the nature treasure box labeled in Braille and stacked neatly in the closet, and Grandfather attached them along the shaft of the cane.

At school, Apu looked forward to his orientation and mobility lessons with Mr. Alan, who came for a couple of days every month to teach him. He proudly reported to his family, "I can get to all the important places in the village with my cane now.

No more holding on to anyone's arm unless I want to."

"What about the teasing?" asked Mother.

"The boys stopped teasing me after Mr. Alan gave each of them a chance to use a cane while they were blindfolded. They weren't very good at it and, some got bruised shins from walking into chairs and sore shoulders from hitting door jambs because they weren't using it right."

Apu felt proud of himself for the first time in a long while. He had ignored the teasing while it lasted and felt a sense of accomplishment. *Maybe not the same level of accomplishment as my ancestors achieved in the wilderness, but I'm only eleven. I have time.*

* * *

After a cold winter, spring arrived and the days were getting lighter. Apu, Brink and Grandfather stood by the water's edge. Mr. Alan had just spent a few days working with Apu and was on his way back to Anchorage. They heard the plane take off from the landing strip with Mr. Alan on board.

Apu commented, "The fog is thick today. I hope the flight goes well."

"How do you know it's foggy? You can't see it," said Brink.

Apu sighed, "You should know by now that there are other ways of seeing, Brink. I can feel the wet on my skin and in my nose, I can smell the tundra soil, and I can hear how muffled the sound of the plane is. In my mind's eye, that means fog."

The boys walked away from the water without touching. Apu used his cane and Brink marched, twirled, and sidestepped beside him. Brink said, "Apu, I didn't know that your freedom to walk by yourself would give me freedom, too."

Apu stopped listening to the tap-tap of his cane and focused on the sound of Brink skipping and Grandfather limping. He smiled at the thought of each having their own sound as they moved. Together, those sounds formed a happy rhythm. The only sound missing was . . . Then he heard it. *There it is.* A loon called a warning.

"Hey Brink, watch for the eagle."

Glossary of Yupik Words

Yupik vocabulary were provided by Marie Meade. Marie is Yup'ik Eskimo from Southwest Alaska. She is a humanities scholar, language expert, and educator and Yup'ik tradition bearer. Meade teaches Central Yup'ik language, orthography and Alaska Native dance at the University of Alaska Anchorage.

CHAPTER 1:
Apa'urluq – Grandfather
Asveq – walrus
Ayaruq – mobility cane
Ciuliat – ancestors
Elitnaurista – teacher
Elitnaurvik - school
Iluracungaq – cousin
Nunapik – Tundra
Nunat – village
Qaleqcuuq – loon
Tengssuun – airplane
Yaqulpak – bald eagle

CHAPTER 2:
Angicissun - tool
Maurluq - Grandmother
Mellgaq – carving knives
Tegganeq – village elder
Tegun - harpoons

CHAPTER 4:
Iinruq – good luck charm
Nunapik – Tundra

CHAPTER 5:
Ataata – Great-Uncle
Cupsaraq - flute
Keglunret – wolves
Manaq – fishing rod
Qimugciurta – musher

CPSIA information can be obtained
at www.ICGtesting.com
Printed in the USA
JSHW022247280322
24363JS00006B/143